M000076478

THIS

NOTEBOOK

BELONGS TO:

DATE:

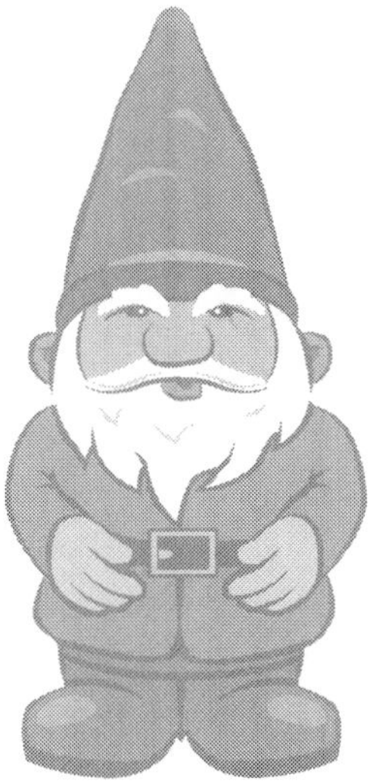

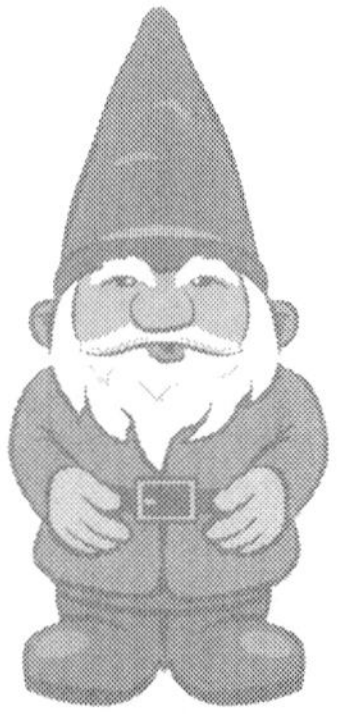

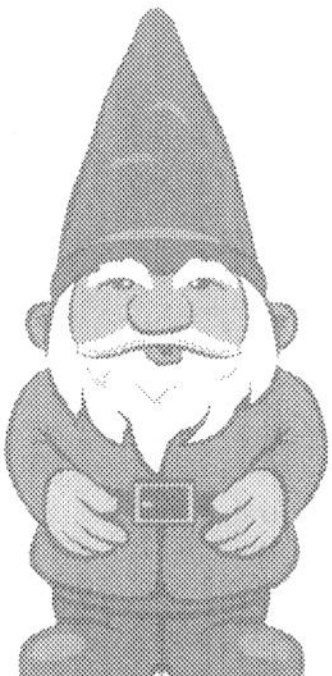

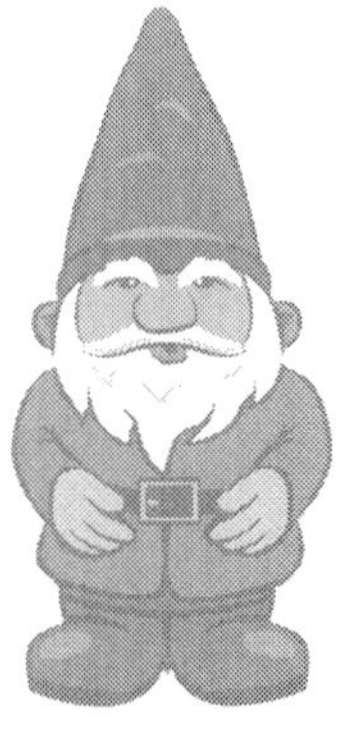

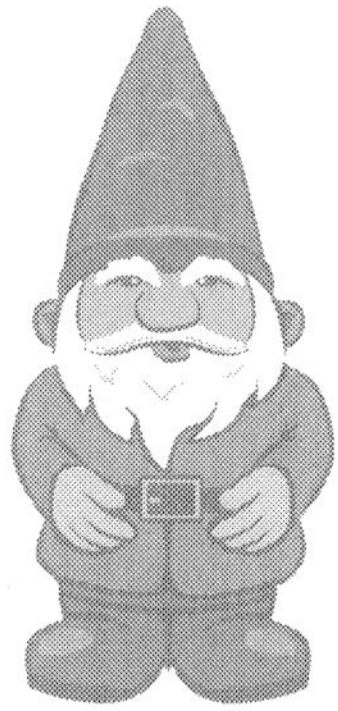

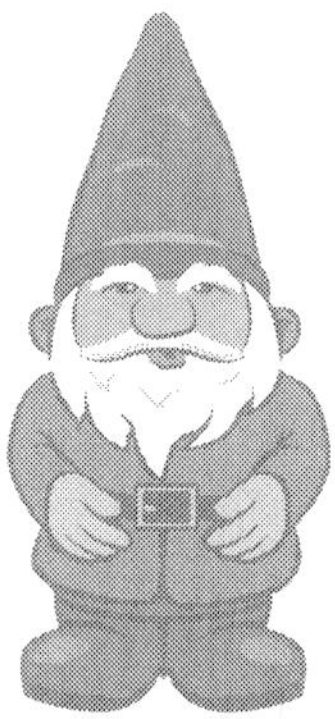

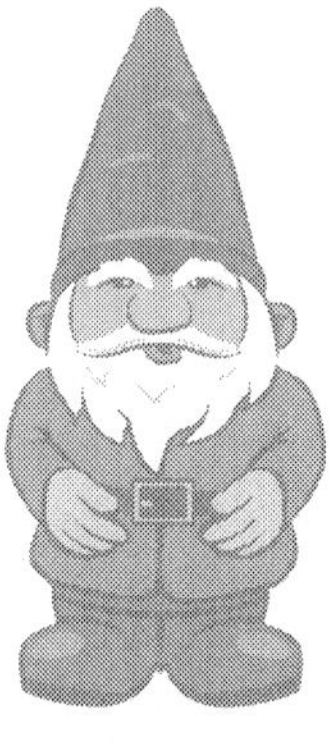

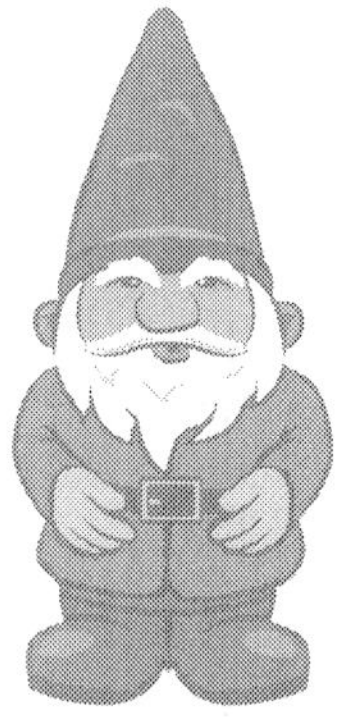

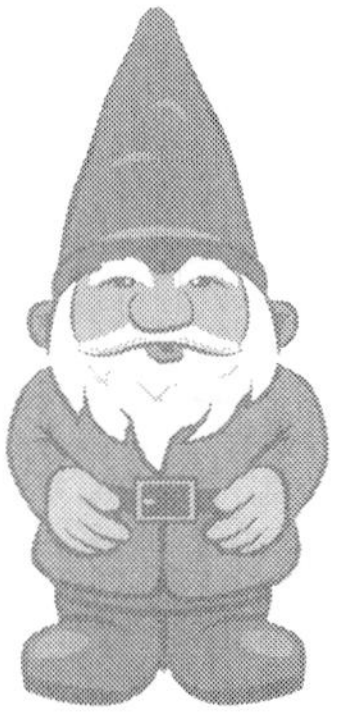

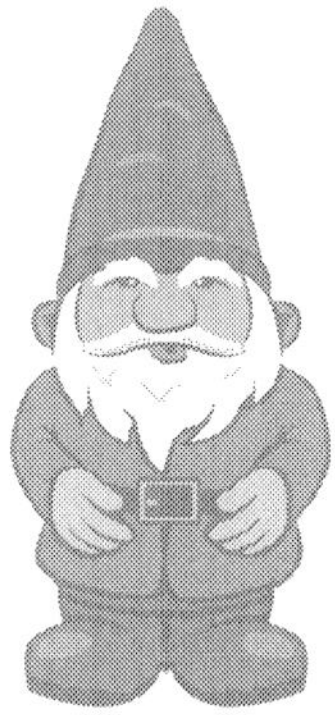

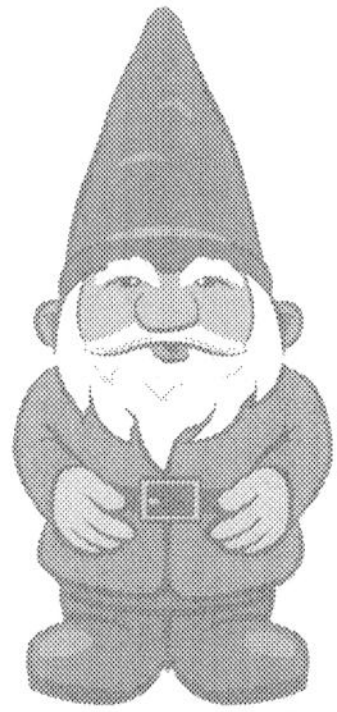

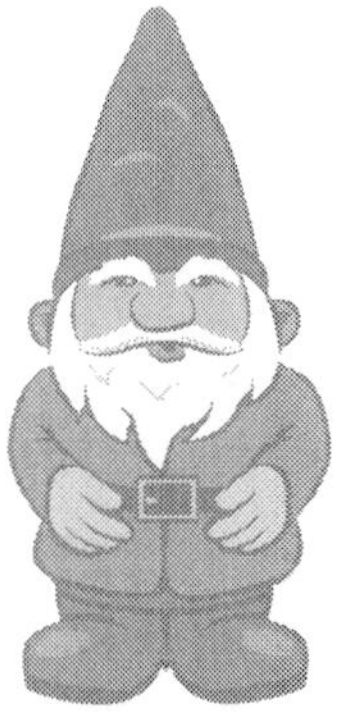

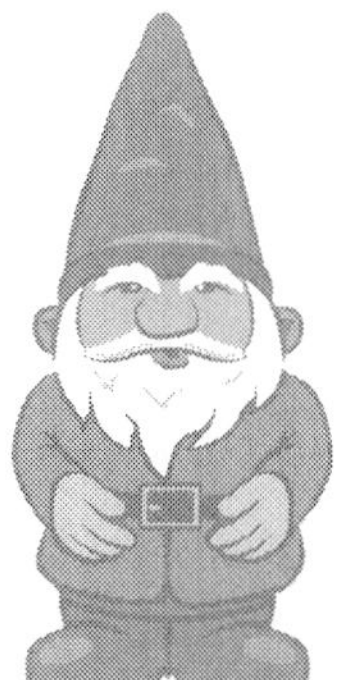

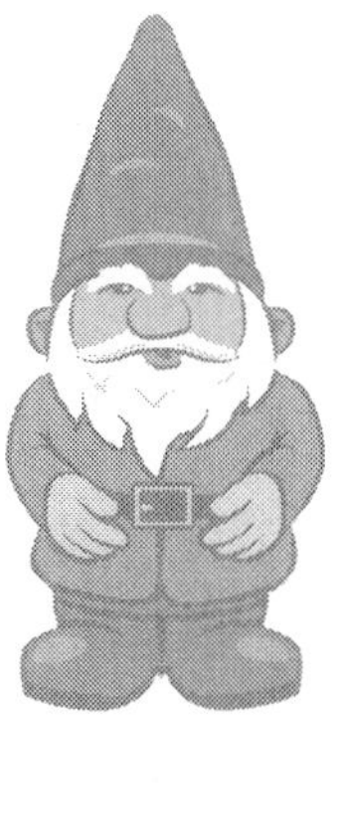

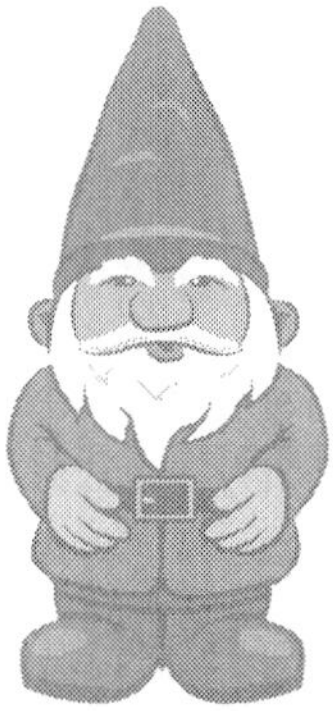

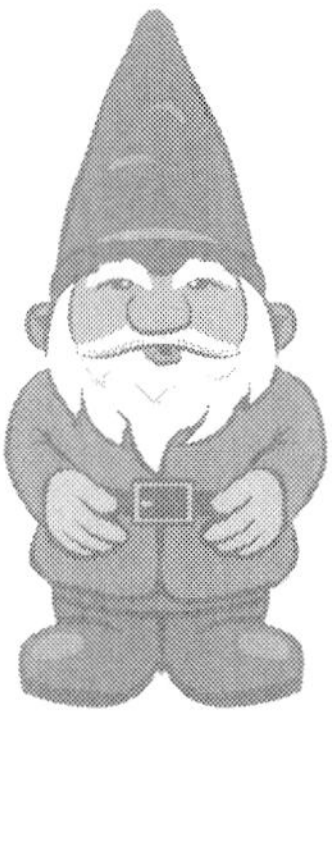

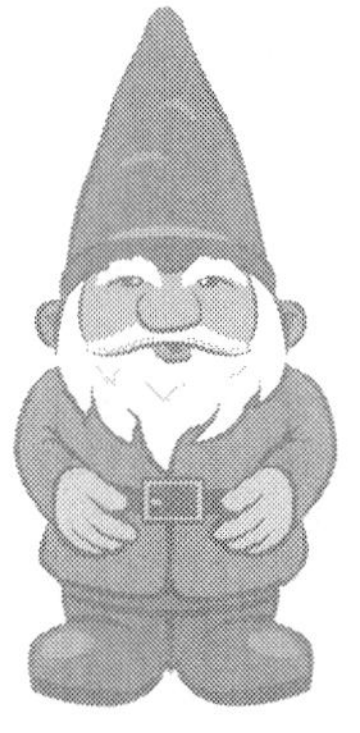

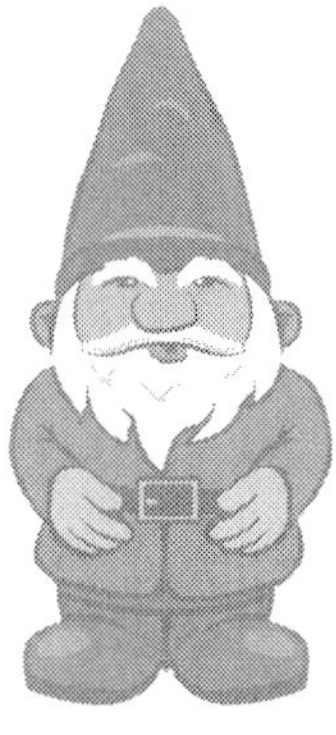

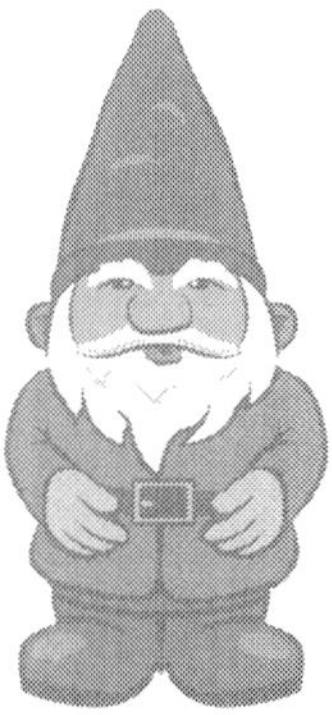

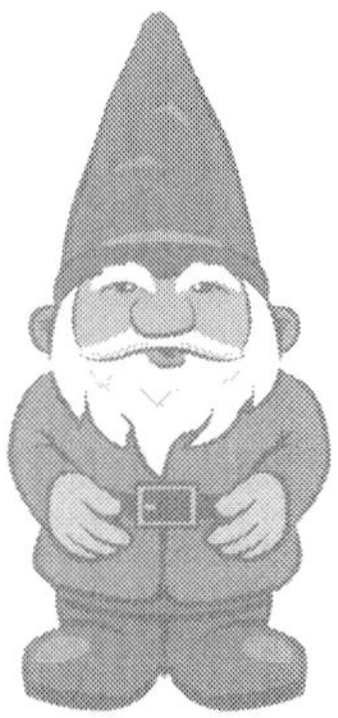

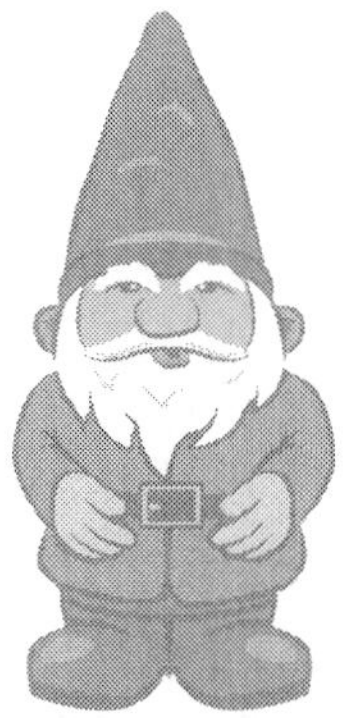

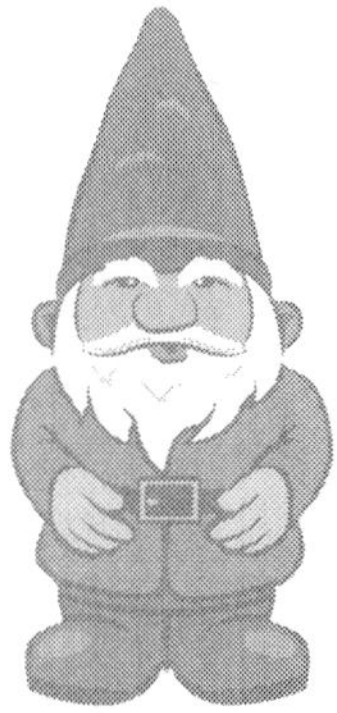

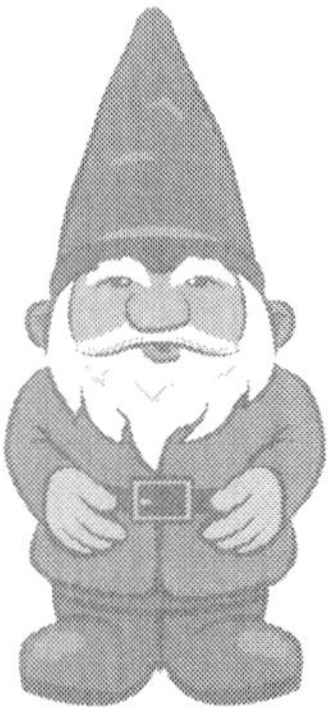

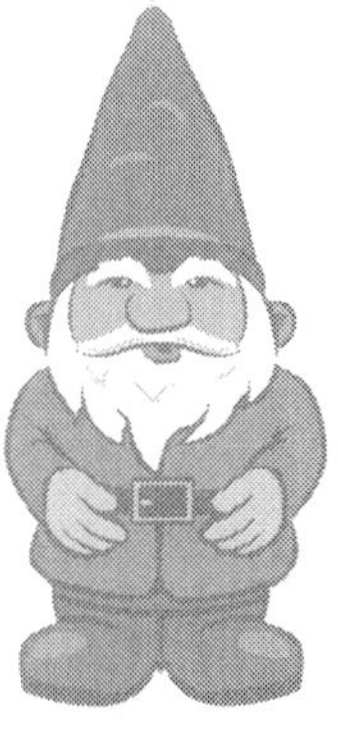

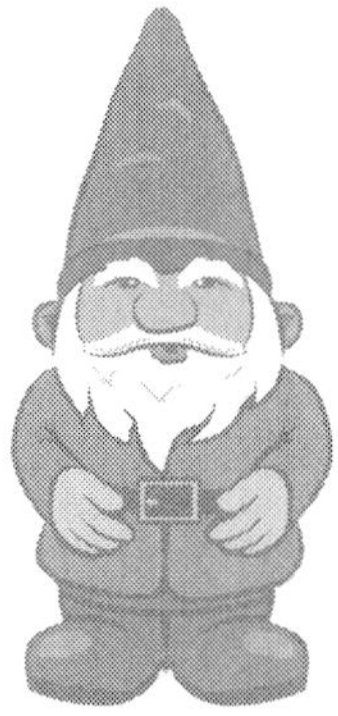

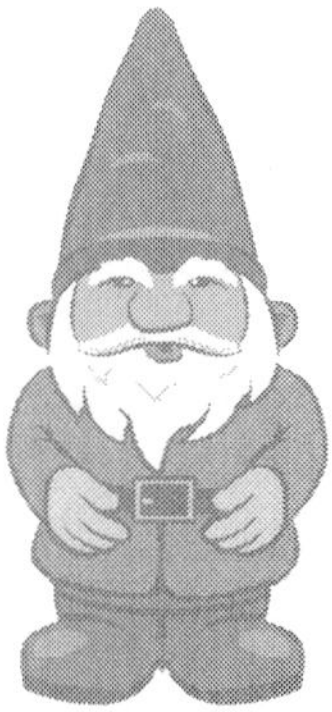

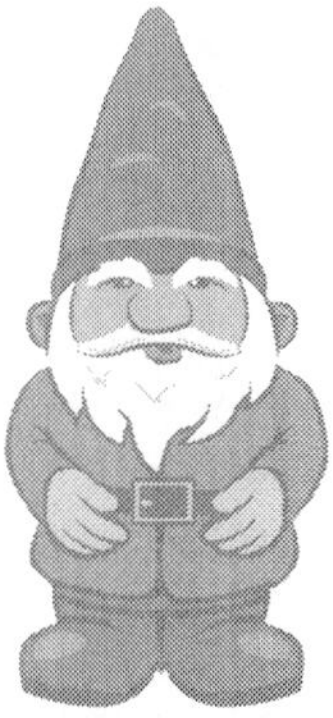

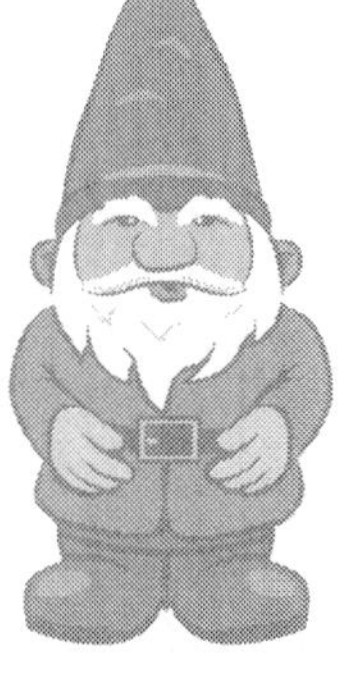

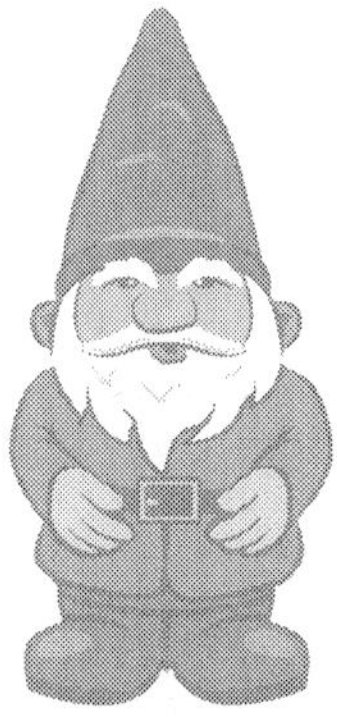

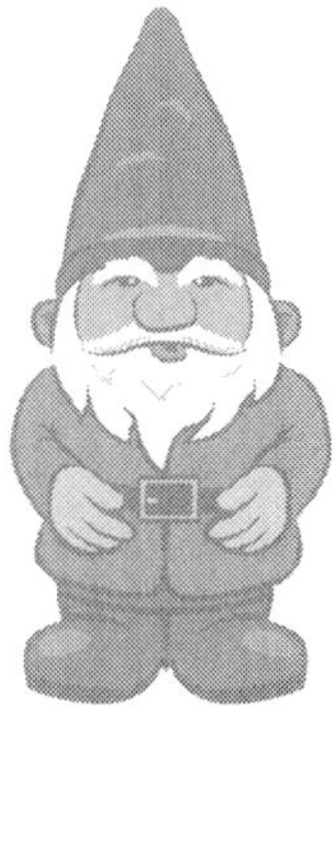

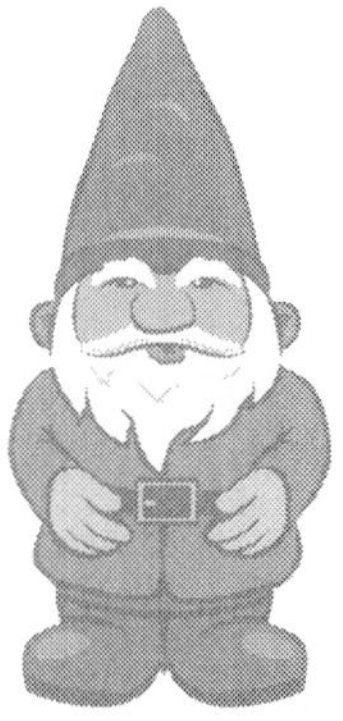

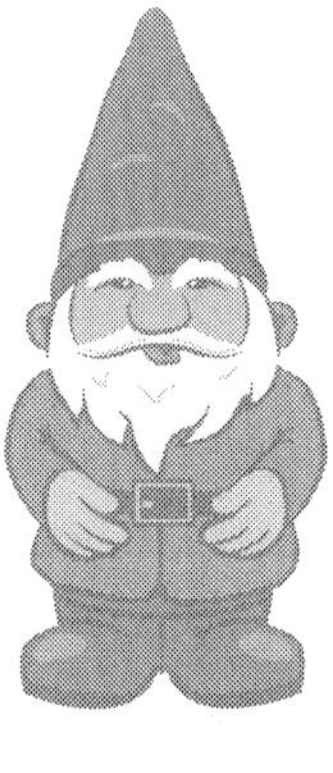

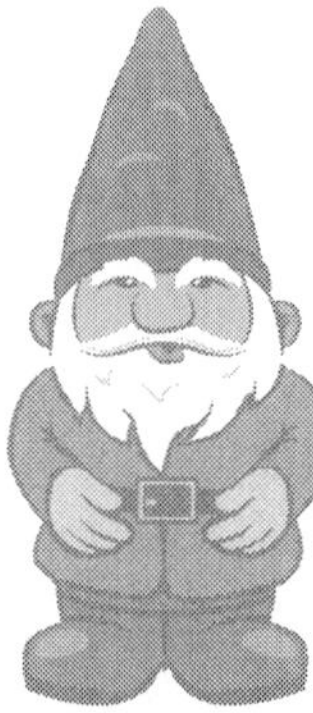

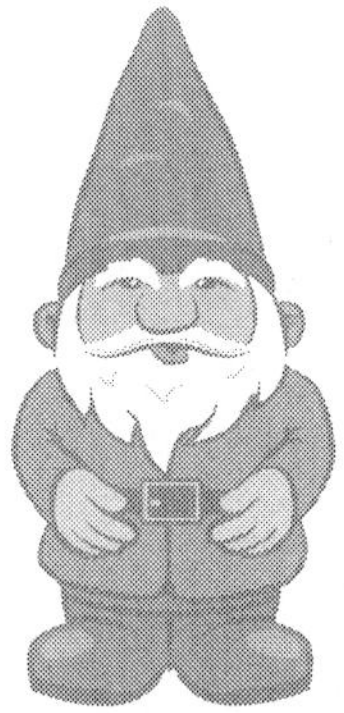

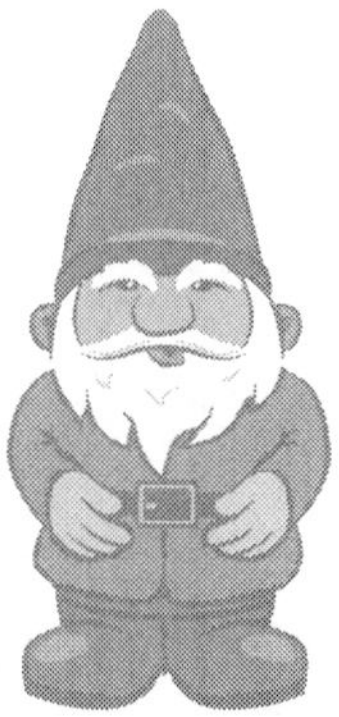

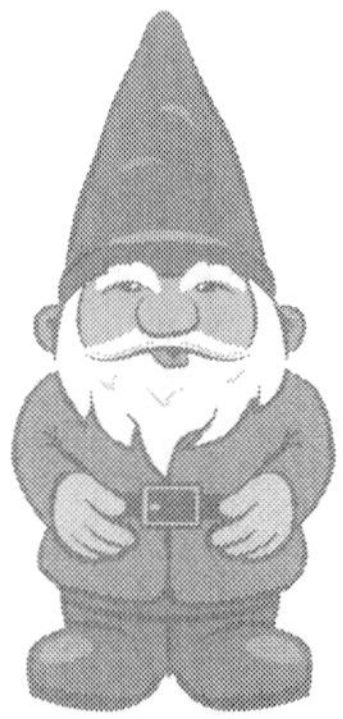

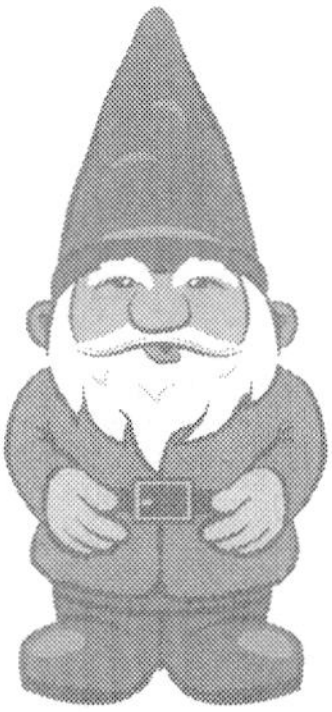

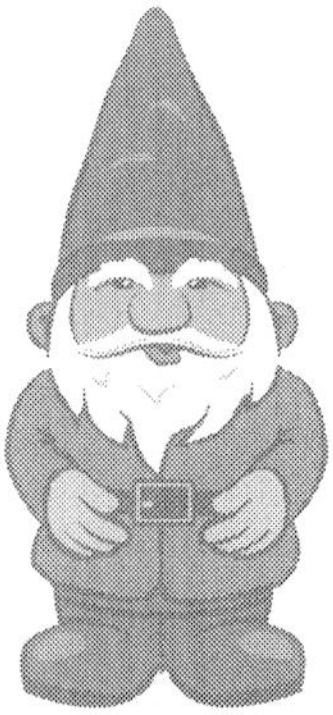

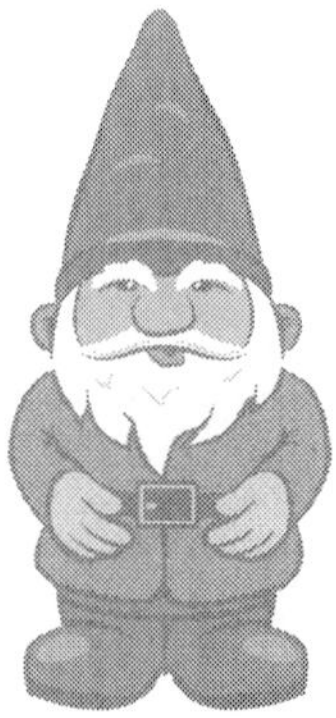

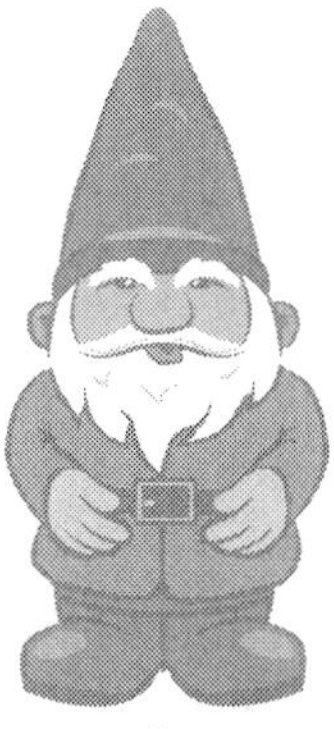

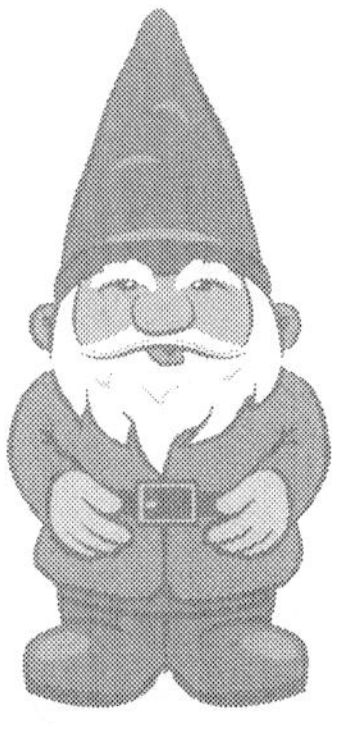

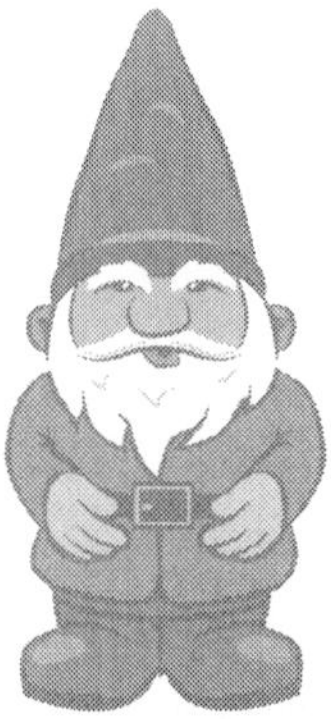

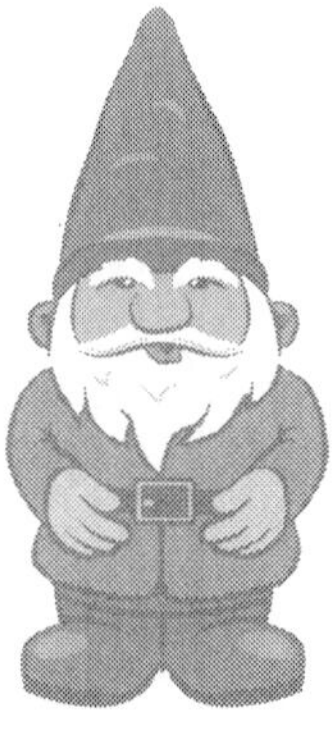

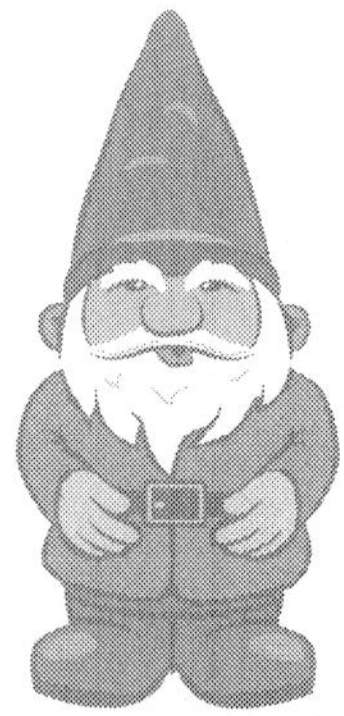

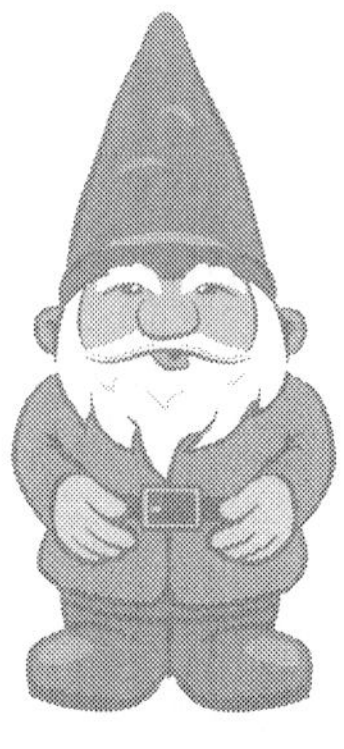

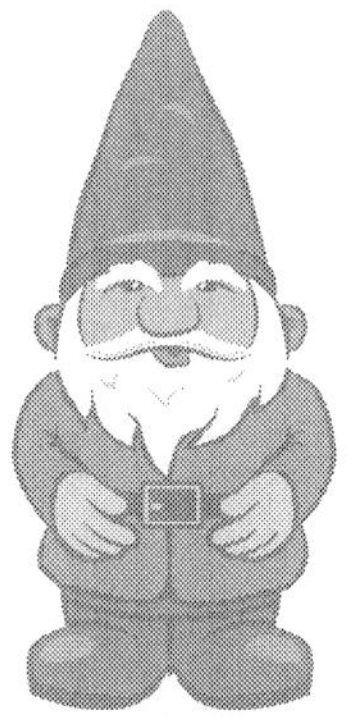

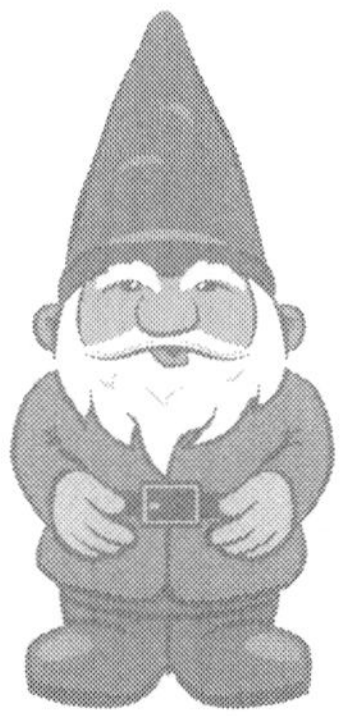

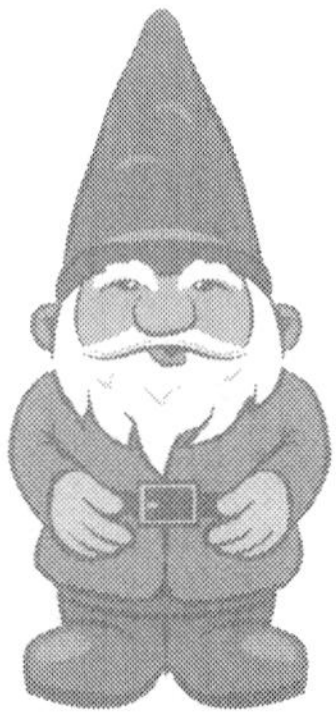

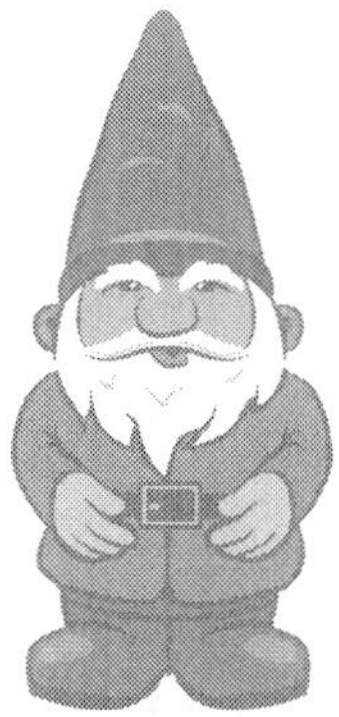

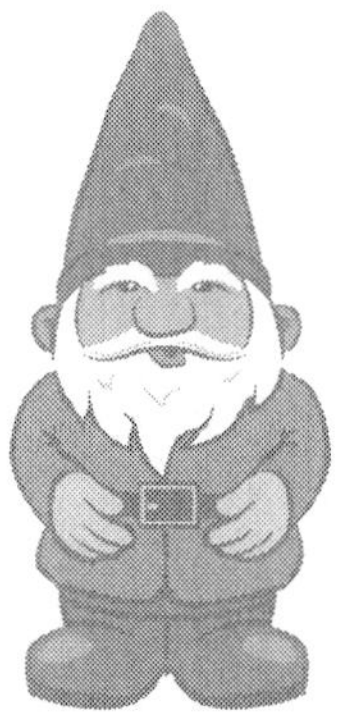

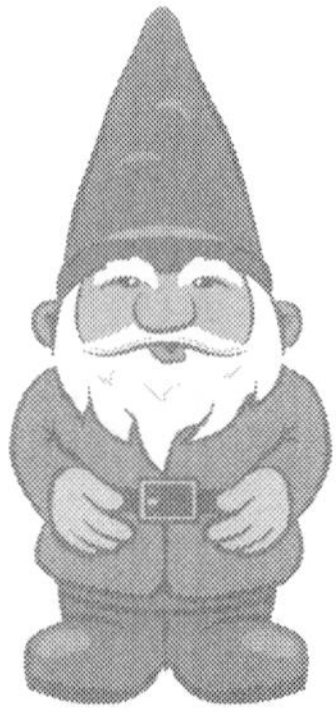

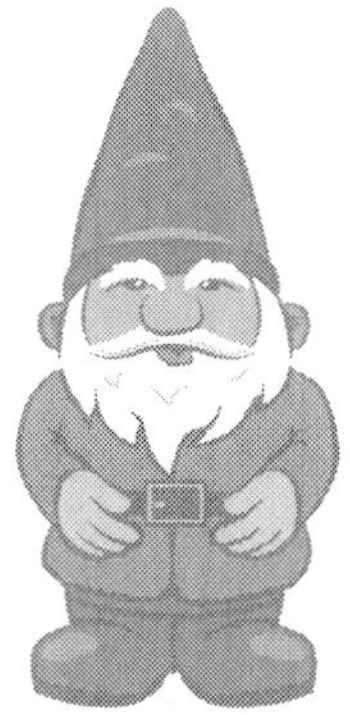

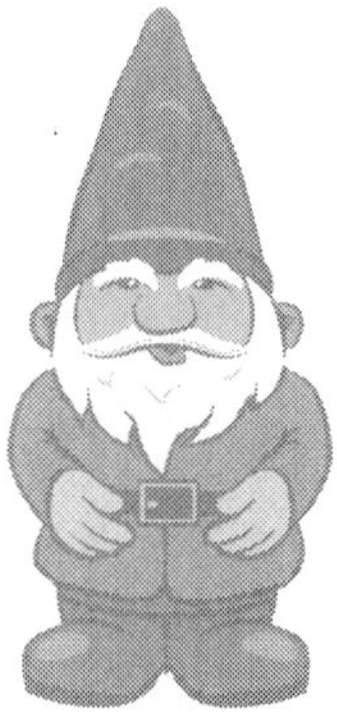

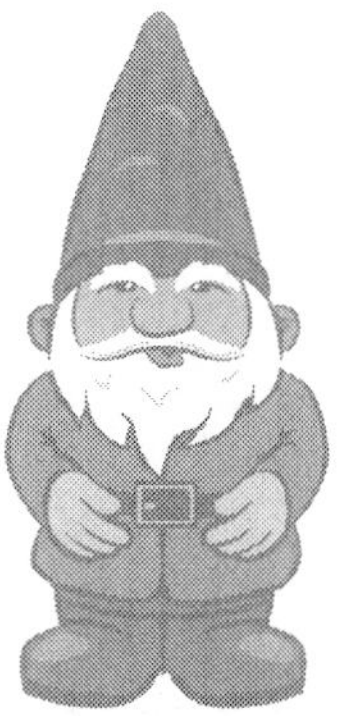

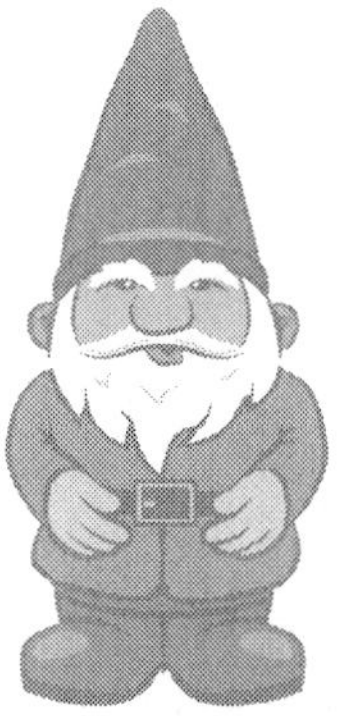

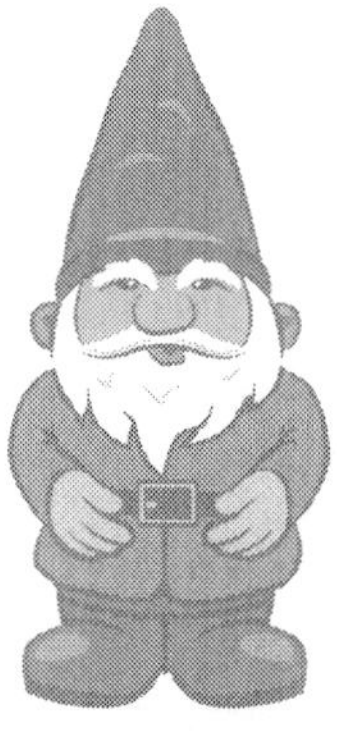

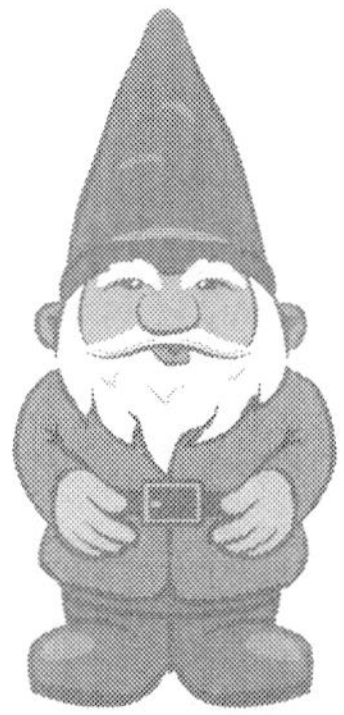

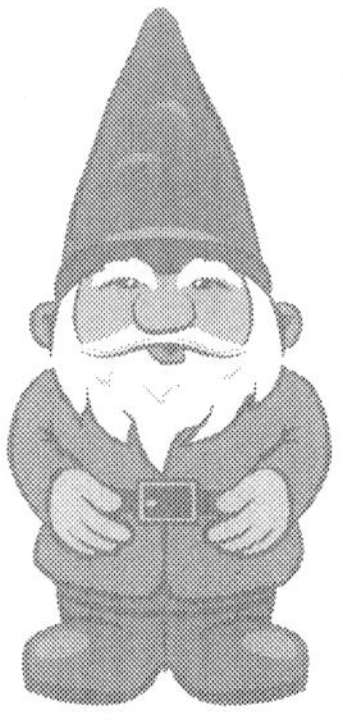

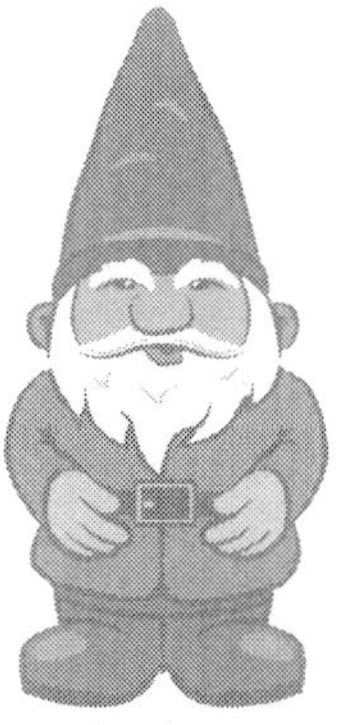

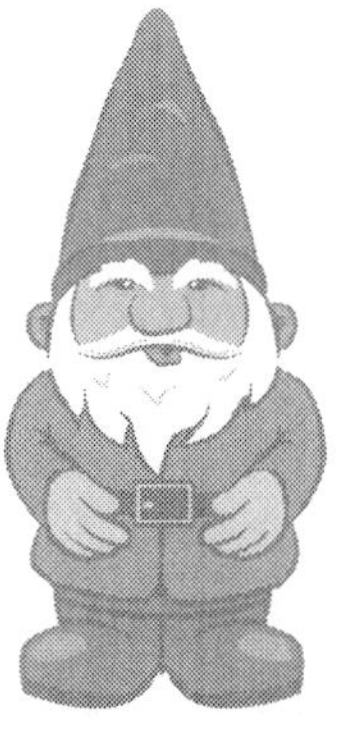

Made in the USA
Columbia, SC
06 May 2021

37451696R00067